# RICE PUBLIC LIBRARY

### KITTERY, MAINE

Copy ························

No. ········· J–F–O ·············

This book may be kept for 14 days. During that time the book may be renewed for another 14 days.

There is a fine of *five* cents per day on any overdue book.

The borrower is liable for any damaged or lost book.

Osborne, Mary Pope          A visit to sleep's house.

# A Visit to Sleep's House

by Mary Pope Osborne
illustrated by Melissa Bay Mathis

Alfred A. Knopf
*New York*

*For my mother*
M.P.O.

*For Shoshana, and for Lundy*
M.B.M.

AUTHOR'S NOTE

*A Visit to Sleep's House* was inspired
by a passage from *Metamorphoses,*
a collection of myths by the Roman
poet Ovid (43 B.C.–A.D. 17).

This is a Borzoi Book
Published by Alfred A. Knopf, Inc.

Book design by Elizabeth Hardie
Manufactured in Singapore

2 4 6 8 0 9 7 5 3 1

Library of Congress Cataloging-in-Publication Data
Osborne, Mary Pope. A visit to Sleep's house.
Summary: A child visits the house of Sleep, where everything is quiet
except for the river that whispers, "Good night, good night."
[1. Sleep—Fiction] I. Mathis, Melissa Bay, ill. II. Title.
PZ7.081167Vi 1989 [E] 88-536 ISBN 0-394-89958-X
ISBN 0-394-99958-4 (lib. bdg.)

Far, far away, on the side of a mountain,
drowsy Sleep lives in a cloud-covered house.

As you walk up Sleep's pathway
no owl calls out, "Who?"
and no dog barks under the moon

In Sleep's starry sky no birds flap their wings.
The wind doesn't blow on Sleep's misty hilltop.

Wild animals don't roar in Sleep's dark woods

The cows don't moo in Sleep's dewy pasture,
and no crickets sing in the grass.

Geese don't cackle when you step into Sleep's yard.
The cat doesn't cry by the gate.

And the hinges don't creak when you enter Sleep's house.
And the floorboards are silent as you walk down Sleep's hall.

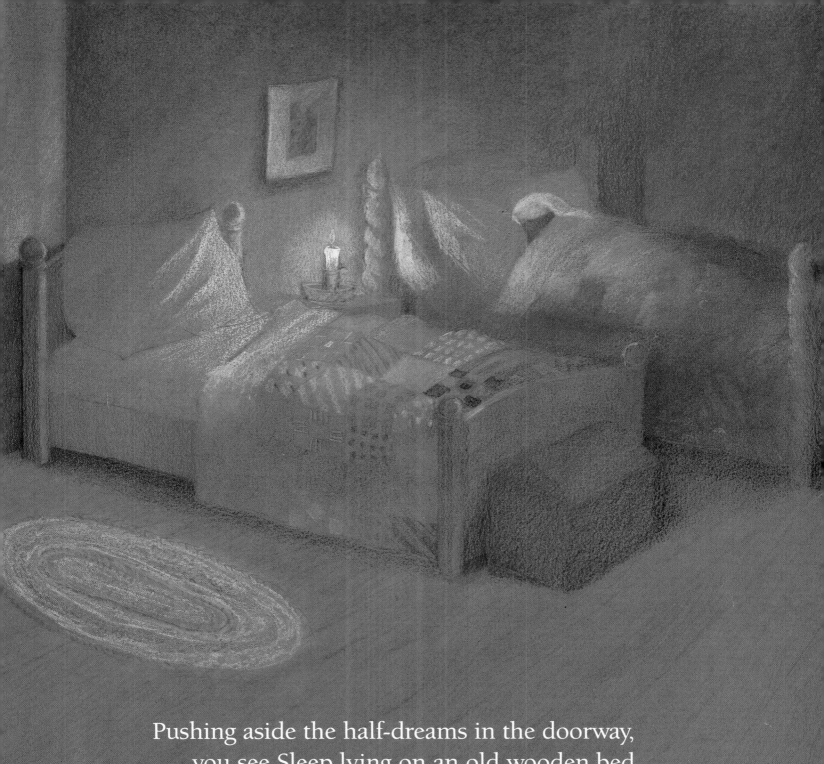

Pushing aside the half-dreams in the doorway,
you see Sleep lying on an old wooden bed.
Beside Sleep's bed is a bed all your own.

You climb into it and pull up a soft feather spread,
and Sleep calms the air in the room.

Then all around you appear different dreams—
as many dreams as leaves in the woods.

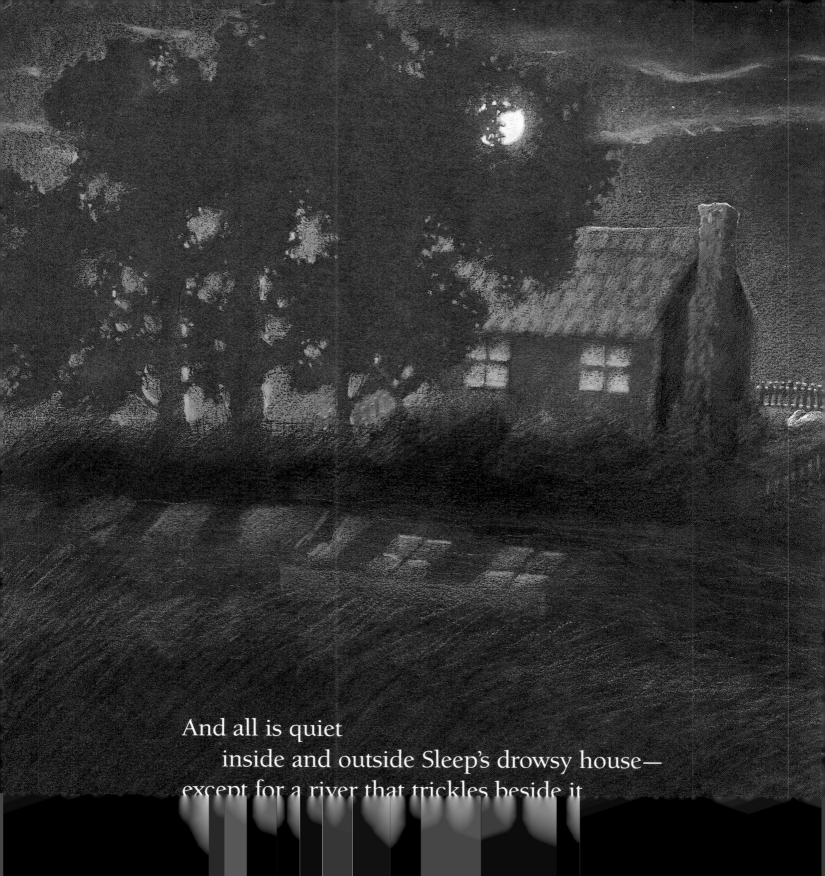

And all is quiet
      inside and outside Sleep's drowsy house—
except for a river that trickles beside it.

and whispers, *Good night, good night.*